PETROLEUM
By
Terence F. Moss

Rapley House. 29 Creek Road
Hayling Island Hampshire PO11 9QZ
Published August 2021

Other works by the author.

Stage Musicals
Angels and Kings
Soul Traders

Pilot TV Comedy's
The Inglish Civil War
Closing Time

Novels
The Prospect of Redemption 2012
The Killing Plan 2013
The Tusitala 2015
Be Happy with my Life 2017

Stage Plays & Adaptations
Better by Far 2018
Petroleum 2021
The Other Life Department 2021

Terence F. Moss
butchmoss@outlook.com
Terence F. Moss on Facebook

Setting.

Ali's Bar is a café/bar on the outskirts of Basra, Iraq. It is 2009. The time is 6pm.

There is a long bar stage right. The room is sparse, the paintwork is greyish/blue and badly needs repainting. The walls are off white with out-of-date posters and signs. The brass foot rails and handrails around the bar are highly polished. There is a large mirror behind the bar. An assortment of bar paraphernalia - Beer pumps - Charity boxes – Small bust of Saddam Hussein with a bowler hat etc. There's a plaque on the wall stating: Est 17AD. Serving the community for nearly 2,000 years. The 2,000 has been crudely changed on several occasions with a magic marker. It now reads 2009.

There is an assortment of spirits on optics behind the bar and an old Jukebox style Coke-a-cola fridge full of beer. There is a meat kebab machine revolving on the back of the bar. The floor is sandy. There is an AMI H120E jukebox in the corner. There are visual reminders of earlier years.

At the back of the set are three doors.
The middle double door is marked EXIT TO REALITY (Invaders – Media – Marketing). There is a second smaller door on the far-right marked EXIT (locals). On the far left is a third door unmarked.

There are four round tables with chairs, they are scattered around the room. There are four bar stools at the bar. The windows are shuttered. Large hanging railway station type light fittings. There are American, English, Jewish, and

Iraqi flags on the wall. As Falls Witchita is playing in the background. (By Pat Metheny).

CHARACTERS.

Shamia

Shia freedom fighter. Everybody calls him “Shaky” Wears a badge / T-shirt which says SHI’ITE. Stands about 6'2" good physique. Age 27. Wearing battle fatigues / terrorist garb. Speaks in broken English.

Akmed

Sunni (Shamia’s brother) freedom fighter thinks he looks like Brad Pitt. Wears jeans and a badge / T-shirt which says SUNNI. Stands about 5'10” medium build. Age 25 and smiles a lot when not asleep.

JJ

US Army Sergeant. He is overweight, about 50.

Walter P. Riddall

Old hack reporter working for CNN. He is an American. Macho, biggish nose looks a little like Karl Malden (American actor) Dresses smart casual despite general conditions. Speaks with a polished Boston accent, his words slur into each other. Age about 50.

Desmond Johns (Dizzie)

Sound/cameraman. He is English working with Walter. Aged about 40. Always carries an umbrella with a Union Jack pattern.

Alistair Barr (Ali)
Ali has a black eye patch, but he has nothing wrong with his eye. Lifts the eye patch up from time to time to see something clearer. Smokes cigars. Age about 35-40.

Morgiana (Max)
English, married to an Iraqi carpet salesman. Attractive, tall, usually a little drunk. Dresses well, age 35.

Shakira
Shamia's wife. Swears a lot in broken English. Attractive women of Iraqi extraction. Dark complexion, long black hair 5'9" Age about 26. They have one child.

Dave
The Redemptor. He has a casual 1960's hippy aura about him.

Scene One opens INT. 6pm

Occasional gunshots, light flashes and explosions can be heard and seen outside the café. The noise can be heard intermittently throughout the play. Ali is polishing a tumbler.

Walter and Dizzie are sitting at a table replaying some film footage from the day. Sundry E.N.G. equipment, mikes, laptops etcetera scattered around the table and floor. They are talking animatedly to each other. JJ is sitting with them, drinking a beer and eating a Kebab.

Akmed is sitting at the bar, apparently asleep.
Morgiana is sitting on her own at the end of the bar drinking a large cocktail.

*Shamia, dressed as an Islamic terrorist, bursts in through the tall double doors marked "*EXIT TO REALITY*." He is brandishing an AK47 assault rifle in one hand. He strikes an iconic pose with his rifle over his head and slowly looks around the room. His entrance is dynamic and highly animated. Background battle sound increases, then slowly fades away.*

SHAMIA

Assalam Alaikum Wa Rahmatullahi Wa Barakatuh. Death to all infidels and non-believers!

Everybody, except Akmed, who is asleep at the bar, glances round to look at Shamia. Ali is standing behind the bar. He looks directly at Shamia, promptly raises his open hand as if reprimanding him.

ALI

Whoa' Shaky... Wa ʿalaykumu s-salam
to you, but you came in the wrong door.

Ali points to the double doors marked **"EXIT to REALITY"** *and another sign above the doors saying* **HOUSE RULE.** *(1).* **"Would all patrons leaving the establishment, kindly exit as quietly as possible as we do not wish to disturb our neighbours. Thank You. The Management."**
The on-stage cast stop what they are doing and slowly turn to look at Shamia.

SHAMIA

What?

ALI

You came in the out door! You should have used that one...
Ali points to the left-hand door marked **"No Exit."**
...I've changed the doors around to avoid confusion.

SHAMIA

Appears confused.
What? Oh, right, sorry Ali, I'll do that again.

Shamia, appearing embarrassed and slightly crestfallen, saunters out through the door marked EXIT TO REALITY. *Battle sounds resume. Everybody else returns to what they were doing. After about ten seconds, he bursts back through the narrower-shorter door marked,* NO EXIT, *once again holding the AK47 high above his head and with what now appears to be sticks of dynamite tied around his chest. This is a less impressive, slightly clumsier stage entrance due to the height of the door. His gun smashes into the top of the doorway. He mumbles, "fuck."*

SHAMIA

Don't nobody move! All Americans must die. I am freedom fighter and ready to serve Allah.

He looks at Ali.

Raise hands and give me coke with absolutely none of your American infidel Pig Dog Bacardi in it!

Ali half-heartedly puts his arms up after placing the glass he is polishing on the bar counter. Everybody else ignores him. The battle sounds fade away.

ALI

Your usual?

SHAMIA

Yes, please.

Spoken quietly

Ali wiggles his hands, still being held aloft and points over his shoulder to the spirits on the shelf behind him.
Shamia gestures with his rifle for Ali to lower his hands.

Ali ostentatiously pours some coke into a glass and tops it up with a tiny dash of Bacardi and pushes the glass across the bar. Shamia moves slowly towards the bar to pick up his drink while looking around the room, attempting to intimidate the other customers. He fails to elicit any response.

ALI

Much, much better Shaky. Centre stage - wrong door, not good. Can you make sure you use the other door next time? It avoids confusion.

Shamia nods his head, appearing to accept Ali's recommendation happily.

SHAMIA

No problem, governor.

ALI

Ali holds up both thumbs and gives Shamia an affectionate nod and a wink.

By the way, I'm not American. They are,

He points at Walter's table. Walter and JJ give Shamia a friendly handwave and a smile.

except for Dizzie; he's British, and the Bacardi's from Jamaica.

Dizzie, holds up his folded umbrella, which has a Union Jack pattern and waves it patriotically.

SHAMIA

Jamaica is American!

ALI

No, technically, it's not, it belongs to Jamaica, and that's part of the West Indies. They have the framework of a parliamentary democratically elected constitution with a hereditary monarch, "the Queen," as their sovereign, but it's only a titular title.

SHAMIA

Titular?

Affecting a mannerism of comprehension.

ALI

Yes.

SHAMIA

Are you sure?

ALI

Yes, of course, I'm sure.

SHAMIA

So, Bacardi's not made in America?

ALI

Nope.

SHAMIA

That's good. I'm glad the imperialistic American bastards haven't taken everything from us poor Muslims. Mind you, the British aren't much better.

WALTER

Hey! no loud or aggressive political rhetoric in the bar, thanks. Especially after the shitty day I've just had. Can't you read?

Walter points to another sign on the wall behind the bar which reads------

HOUSE RULES. (2)

To preserve this establishment's quiet and peaceful ambience, we politely request that all customers kindly refrain from using loud or aggressive political or religious rhetoric or chanting seditious Mantra's while drinking in the bar area. Thank You. The Management.

SHAMIA

What?

Shamia appears dumbfounded by the sign.

ALI

Sorry, Shaky. House rule!

Ali points to the sign behind the bar and makes a grimacing expression at Shamia. WALTER gives Shamia a slight nod and a wink. Dizzie gives Shamia a knowing smile. Morgiana looks up, smiles at Shamia, and waves her cocktail.

SHAMIA

House rule?

SHAMIA appears overwhelmed by the rule and takes a swig of his Bacardi and Coke.

ALI

House rule! Sorry, things have changed
a little since you were last here.

SHAMIA

Oh! Since when?

Shamia sounds surprised and drops his gun on the bar. Takes another sip from his glass of Bacardi and Coke and then places it back on the bar.

ALI

Since you were last in… obviously.

Ali carries on polishing a tumbler.

SHAMIA

SHAMIA pushes his glass back across the counter and whispers…

Less Coke, please. Infidel!

ALI

Less Coke?

Ali looks confused for a few moments, then puts more Bacardi in the glass and passes it back. Shamia tastes the drink.

SHAMIA

Getting better.

He passes the drink back to Ali again after a few moments.

ALI

Less?

SHAMIA

Please.

Ali smiles and pours three-quarters of the coke away while Shamia is looking around the bar. He pours in more Bacardi. It is now nearly transparent. He puts the drink back on the bar and pushes it over to SHAMIA. SHAMIA turns around, picks it up and takes a sip.

SHAMIA

That's much better, thank you.

Shamia places the drink on the bar top and continues looking around the room and at the ceiling.

ALI

Good…

ALI

Ali pauses for a few moments deliberating on whether he should continue with something that is obviously troubling him.

Tell me something?

SHAMIA

Anything, my little Hebrew friend.

Shamia flashes Ali an inquisitorial expression.

ALI

I'm not Jewish and I'm not little.

Ali lifts his eye patch momentarily and glares at Shamia. Ali appears slighted.

SHAMIA

Are you sure? You look Jewish?

ALI

Yes.

SHAMIA

No trimming of the ehh… excess?

He points towards his crutch area then makes a snipping gesture.

ALI

No, not in my religion, not necessary.

Ali grins

SHAMIA

Pauses

It stops you from going mad, you know.

ALI

Does it?

SHAMIA

Absolutely. Look at me?

ALI

I am.

SHAMIA

He pauses before continuing.

You're sure you're not/

ALI

/Yes, of course, I am. And by the way, I thought the consumption of alcohol was forbidden by your lot?

SHAMIA

Shamia leans in a little closer to Ali and holds up a tutorial finger and waggles it.

Absolutely. It does! But then none of this is real, is it, so it doesn't really matter.

SHAMIA

Shamia shrugs at the audience, smiles at Ali again and tilts his head to one side before bringing it back to upright. He takes another sip of the Bacardi.

It's very lovely.

ALI

Good…good… so, why now, after all this time?

SHAMIA

I thought I would try it while I had the chance… for political and theological research purposes, you understand.

Shamia flashes Ali a smile.

JJ and Walter look over inquisitorially at the mention of the "political" word

ALI

And?

SHAMIA

I like it.

ALI

So, you've never drunk it before, and now you find you like it despite vehemently denouncing it for the last thirteen hundred years.

SHAMIA

Well, that's not strictly accurate, and it wasn't just me. There are quite a lot of us, you know.

ALI

I know.

SHAMIA

And I have been here before… many times.

ALI

I know. You are one of my best customers, but you never drank alcohol before.

SHAMIA

In a manner of speaking.

ALI

What do you mean, a manner of speaking?

SHAMIA

I did have it before. I just didn't buy it.

ALI

So, who did?

SHAMIA

Morgiana.

ALI

Morgiana?

They both look over to Morgiana sitting at the end of the bar, and she gives them both a tiny wave and a smile before holding up her cocktail and taking a sip.

SHAMIA

Yes.

ALI

For you?

SHAMIA

Yes.

ALI

Why?

SHAMIA

Because I like it, but for the sake of appearance, I thought it best not to be seen buying it.

ALI

So, are you a Muslim just for the sake of appearance?

SHAMIA

No

With indignation and surprise

ALI

But you are openly buying it now?

SHAMIA

I didn't feel comfortable being part of a hypocritical ethnic charade.

ALI

So now you are being honest with yourself about your true feelings. Maybe you aren't really a Muslim after all?

SHAMIA

No, I'm Muslim. I just like Bacardi.

ALI

What would the Grand Mufti say about that?

SHAMIA

Ayatollah. The Mufti's his lot

Shamia nods to his brother Akmed.

ALI

Ayatollah then. So, what would he say?

SHAMIA

Not a lot. Probably issue a fatwa condemning me to death. That would be an end to the matter.

ALI

Looking surprised at Shamia's benign resignation.

But you would be dead?

SHAMIA

No. not really. It's just a nasty slap on the wrist. He will forgive eventually. Just likes to make you sweat a bit.

ALI

Oh! So why the sudden change of heart?

SHAMIA

It's not just a change of heart - I am simply starting out on a voyage of discovery into the strange ways of the non-believers so I can better understand the differences between us and hopefully arrive at a plateau of understanding and peaceful co-existence where we can all live together in harmony and pacific accord.

ALI

Well, that sounds very encouraging, but it also has the unpleasant whiff of bullshit about it.

SHAMIA

Why?

ALI

When you came in, you said you were a freedom fighter ready to die for Allah, advocating death to the infidels and non-believers, which sort of gave me the impression you were a dedicated Islamic terrorist prepared to die for what you believe.

SHAMIA

I am a freedom fighter; actually, I'm not a terrorist, but I'm having a couple of hours off now. I'm bleeding knackered, running around dodging Yankee bullets all day, and I needed a drink… have you been out there lately?

An expression of alarm flashes across his face. He nods to the outside.

ALI

Nope.

SHAMIA

It's not nice.

ALI

Isn't it?

Still polishing a tumbler.

SHAMIA
Let me tell you, it's bloody dangerous. Nobody knows what's really going on. You could easily be killed. I nearly had my dick shot off when I was having a piss. Those Yankee snipers are sick in the head.

beat

ALI
So, what are you now, some sort of part-time peacemaker?

SHAMIA
Well, I wouldn't go quite that far, more, let's say, of an interested party.

ALI
Interested party?

SHAMIA
Yes, well, I do live here with my family, you know.

ALI
I didn't.

SHAMIA

Used to be a very upmarket neighbourhood when we moved in. Close to the schools and the mosque, house prices rising nicely, expanding economy, good job in the supermarket, I was the assistant manager on the deli counter.

ALI

So, what happened?

SHAMIA

Shamia looks directly at Ali, apparently stunned by the question.

What happened?

There is a large mortar explosion just outside. He points over his shoulder while taking another sip of his drink.

That's what happened.

ALI

Well, you started it.

SHAMIA

No, not me personally. I was having a quiet Sunday barbie with some friends in the garden when this lot kicked off, so don't blame me.

Shamia is indignant.

ALI

So, who did start it?

SHAMIA

Who knows, probably the Americans, they start everything else.

He holds both his hands out, palms up.

ALI

But you did join in?

SHAMIA

Didn't have much of an option. They…

He points at JJ, and Walter

flattened the supermarket and the school on day one. House prices have been plummeting ever since. I had to do something.

WALTER

Hey, don't blame me. I'm just a newsman and a neutral observer for CNN; I didn't start anything.

SHAMIA

Everybody's a neutral observer. It's a real mystery how anything started.

Hint of sarcasm

ALI

So, that's why you became a terrorist?

SHAMIA

I prefer freedom fighter, if you don't mind!

ALI

Sorry, freedom fighter.

SHAMIA

It has a better buzz.

ALI

Ali nods

So, what happens when you go back to your fundamentalistic comrades? How do you explain that?

Ali points at the Bacardi.

SHAMIA

Explain what?

ALI

Why you were drinking Bacardi with some Americans in a bar of ill repute.

SHAMIA

I will just say it was a mistake and condemn the Bacardi as the vomit of American pig dog capitalism; that should cut it.

ALI

Little bit more hypocrisy going on there.

SHAMIA

Not really, just intermingling, merging in if you like … absorbing the culture, and doing a little research into the mentality of the oppressors. When in Rome and all that…

ALI

This isn't Rome.

SHAMIA

No, I know that, but you know what I mean?

ALI

Not really

Ali shrugs.

SHAMIA

To Ali spoken quietly, almost whispered with a hint of indignation.

When I came in, you said there were new house rules. What's that all about?

ALI

That's right, there are, now… No political or religious rhetoric in the bar can be very unsettling for the other customers. There are a few other rules as well.

Ali points at the sign again behind him.

SHAMIA

But I don't do house rules, I'm a freedom fighter, and I'm/

CAST

Everybody except Ali chants half-heartedly...

"Ready to die for Allah", yes, we know.

Shamia looks surprised by the mantra.

WALTER

Mutters.

/And a Terrorist!

ALI

Ali to everybody and pointing at the sign.

No mantras in the bar, thank you!

Everybody acknowledges his request by waving their hands.

SHAMIA

Shamia looks a little disturbed by the casual disregard for his mantra and curiously asks.

No Mantras?

ALI

Ali points to the "No Political Rhetoric at any time!" sign.

Yep, it's a/

SHAMIA

/don't tell me, House rule, I get it.

ALI

So why don't you sit down, drink your Coke, and chill out? Be friendly to my customers. You heard what Walter said - he's had a shitty day.

Ali takes a puff on a cigar he has just lit, turns around, spits in a spittoon, turns back and blows cigar smoke over the bar.

SHAMIA

Shamia moves back and quickly puts his hand over his mouth, adopting an expression of abject offence and then coughs.

SHAMIA

But why should I be pleasant? You know the rhetoric?
They are all capitalistic pigs, exploiting our quixotic society's loving and harmonious nature to orchestrate and facilitate unencumbered access to my people's mineral wealth. I am a terrorist fighting for my country.

He picks up his rifle and waves it around menacingly.
Ali gestures to Shamia to put his gun down.

WALTER

I thought you said you were a freedom fighter.

SHAMIA

What?

WALTER

Looking up from his laptop.

When you first came in, you said you were a freedom fighter, now you say you are a terrorist, so, which is it?

SHAMIA

What do you mean, which is it? … its whatever I said I was, I am. I don't have to make choices. I am, who I am, I am a free man. It's your fault you keep confusing me.

WALTER

Sorry Shaky, didn't mean to upset you. I just want to clarify the distinction to avoid any possible confusion or ambiguity in the obituary I'm writing.

DIZZIE

Absolute mon brav, we don't need any more confusion.

SHAMIA

What?

WALTER

Confusion?

SHAMIA

Confusion! confusion over what?

WALTER

The obituary, I was just making some notes for it when/

SHAMIA

/Who's obituary?

WALTER

Yours.

SHAMIA

Mine, oh, I see... Did you spell my name correctly? It's Shamia Mushtichee that's M. U. S. H. T. I. C. H. E. E Hussein

(Shamia walks over to WALTER, leans over his shoulder, and spells out his surname.)

Two "E's," please. Everybody makes that mistake.

WALTER

No problem, two E's.

SHAMIA

Thank you…

Paused puzzlement.

So, what is an obituary?

WALTER

It's a short notice we put in the newspaper. To tell the world what a wonderful person you were and what marvellous things you did.

SHAMIA

That sounds nice. I look forward to reading it.

DIZZIE

You can't; that's unlucky.

SHAMIA

I will read it later then.

DIZZIE

You can't read it later either.

SHAMIA

Can't read it later, why not?

DIZZIE

Because my fanatical friend, you will be in thousands of tiny little pieces by the time they publish it.

SHAMIA

I don't understand, I will/

WALTER

/You will be a dead terrorist.

SHAMIA

Freedom fighter.

WALTER

Whatever.

SHAMIA

Shamia appears shocked by the revelation.

I see.

MORGIANA

I will miss you Shaky. Such a waste.

Morgiana blows him a kiss from the end of the bar.

SHAMIA

My death will not be in vain. I give it freely for my country, my people and Allah.

He hoists his gun above his head and holds an iconoclastic pose for a few moments.

MORGIANA

What about your wife?

SHAMIA

Oh yes, and for my beautiful wife, Shakira.

He relaxes.

MORGIANA

And little Abdulla.

SHAMIA

Yes, and my son Abdulla as well.

ALI

('Ali gestures to Shamia to stop waving his gun about)

DIZZIE

It says here you come from Milton Keynes.

Dizzie is staring at his laptop screen.

SHAMIA

What?

DIZZIE

Milton Keynes, that's where you come from… according to Wikipedia.

Dizzie looks up from his laptop for a response.

SHAMIA

And?

DIZZIE

It also says you were related to a royal family from Persia.

SHAMIA

Does it?

DIZZIE

And it says you have unencumbered access to your family's mineral wealth.

SHAMIA
And?

WALTER
Milton Keynes doesn't have any mineral wealth.

DIZZIE
Unless you count concrete.

SHAMIA
Wikipedia isn't perfect. They do make mistakes.

DIZZIE
But you told us your family run a Kebab takeaway in Newport Pagnell.

SHAMIA
Well, they do now, but originally, we came from Persia. We were princes of the desert.

J.J.
Did you know Lawrence?

SHAMIA
Lawrence? Lawrence who?

JJ
Lawrence of Arabia.

SHAMIA

No, I didn't know fucking Lawrence of Arabia.

Sounding very indignant.

JJ

He got on well with your lot.

SHAMIA

Shamia glances at JJ, appearing stunned and confused by this statement.

My lot? Who the hell are my lot?

JJ

Muzzies, sorry Muslims.

SHAMIA

My lot, I see… well, no, he was a little before my time, actually. Anyway, he was neutral as far as I remember. Got on well with everybody - he rode his camel down the middle of the road, you might say. He just didn't like Turks.

WALTER

Did they have roads in the desert?

SHAMIA

No, they didn't have roads. That was just an analogy

Shamia is looking a little distressed by the conversation

MORGIANA

I have an allergy… to camels.

Everybody turns to look at Morgiana. They appear confused by what she has just said and, in chorus, repeat...

CAST

Camels.

MORGIANA

They bring me out in hives

SHAMIA

Hives?

MORGIANA

Red bumps all over my body if I get near a camel.

SHAMIA

Completely confused by the conversation

What the f…

MORGIANA

I thought he had a camel.

Morgiana now looks surprised and a little confused over their reaction.

JJ

Who?

MORGIANA

Lawrence.

JJ

He did.

MORGIANA

There you are. I knew I was right. It will be his fault if I go all blotchy.

She starts checking her skin.
Everybody else is speechless for a moment.

JJ

He's dead now.

MORGIANA

Surprised.

Is he?

JJ

Died years ago.

MORGIANA

Oh.

SHAMIA waves away more of Ali's cigar smoke.

SHAMIA

There should be a rule about smoking in here. It's incredibly unhealthy. Have you read the Health Department statistics on passive smoking?

ALI

Shakes his head

SHAMIA

There's a 23% chance of contracting lung cancer and dying prematurely if you regularly frequent a smoky environment.

ALI

But you said you were ready to die for Allah.

SHAMIA

I am, but not of bloody lung cancer… Anyway, why all the questions about my family?

WALTER

Just packing the obit out to make it enjoyable. It needs to be a fun read.

SHAMIA

A fun read? Isn't it supposed to be reverent and respectful? I don't want everybody pissing themselves with laughter.

WALTER

Bit cliched, sombre obits. Thought I would jolly it up a bit. Do you have any amusing anecdotes you would like me to include? Anything with sheep would be good; it always goes done well.

SHAMIA

No. no, I don't. I'm not a fucking shepherd. I'm a freedom fighter, that's it!

WALTER

Definitely not a terrorist then?

SHAMIA

No.

WALTER

Right.

Walter makes exaggerated gesture correcting what he has noted down.

It all goes quiet for about twenty seconds…………………

SHAMIA

To Walter

Enjoyable?

WALTER

Sorry?

SHAMIA

You said the obit needs to be amusing and enjoyable?

WALTER

Yes.

SHAMIA

Should it be enjoyed if I have just died?

WALTER

Well, there's no point in moping around for days; what's that going to achieve? So, I thought we could cheer things up a bit and maybe have a party or something.

SHAMIA

You do know I will be dead?

WALTER

There's no need to go on about it. That sort of talk can really suck all the fun out of a party. It was your choice.

SHAMIA

But….

WALTER

Own it. Enjoy the moment.

WALTER

In a philosophical tone, he asks.

Do you realise that if there was only one God or no God at all for that matter, we could have avoided two thousand years of bloodshed?

SHAMIA

Well, scrap yours, and the job is done.

WALTER

That's precisely the narrow-minded bigoted attitude I expect from your lot.

SHAMIA

Muslims are not bigots.

He reaches for his gun again.

WALTER

Yes you are. You're just a bunch of dogmatic left-wing reactionary fascist extremists who got lucky. As for the "gentle harmony of your quixotic society," well, that's a load of old camel shit. You've been shooting the crap out of each other and everybody else since Mohammed popped his sandals, so it's not exactly all milk and honey like you make out……. and you would have probably made shish kebabs out of the donkey if you'd had half a chance.

SHAMIA

Looking confused

What Donkey?

WALTER

The one that Jesus rode to Jerusalem… on Easter Sunday… after the resurrection.

SHAMIA

Wistfully

Now that was a good trick, I'll give you that. Even Mohammed never made it back for a final farewell tour.

WALTER

You know, in some ways, Mohammed was a lot like Jesus. They could even have been the same person if it wasn't for the donkey and about six hundred years.

SHAMIA

That is blasphemy… I can feel a head chop fatwa coming on.

WALTER

Can't I even have an opinion? You must admit, it does make a lot of sense.

SHAMIA

Make sense? How do you work that one out?

Shamia appears confused

WALTER

Well, they were both prophets of a "God."

He does air quotes on God

… and they both died tragically… relatively young.

AKMED

And they were both killed by Jews.

The bar goes quiet, and everybody looks over at Akmed, who has just woken up.

SHAMIA

What?

AKMED.

Jews killed them both. One was crucified, and one was poisoned. I thought everybody knew that.

Everybody looks at Ali.

And Jesus was Jewish and King of the Jews, and still, they didn't cut him any slack.

ALI

Don't look at me. I've told you already, I'm not Jewish; I was a closet Christian in those days.
And anyway, it was very much a bi-partisan political environment. The Romans crucified him, not the Jews. But then they'd crucify anybody regardless of religious inclination if they had a mind to.

AKMED

I understood it was an urgent request from a Jewish delegation because he was a radical left-wing extremist, preaching egregious sedition, not unlike what's happening now with us.

ALI

I don't know about that. I wasn't there, well no, come to think of it. I was there actually, in the general vicinity, you understand, but only in a professional capacity, running the sushi bar.

JJ

As I remember, he upset some bankers and kicked them out of the temple; it all went downhill from there.

AKMED

Bankers have got a lot to answer for.

JJ

Absolutely Mon Brav.

AKMED

I remember that bit from my Sunday school.

JJ

Sunday school? Muslims go to Sunday school?

AKMED

No Christians do. I was a Christian once until I converted to Islam, they see a lot more action, and you meet a different class of people in the mosque.

JJ

Right, I see.

He looks a little bewildered

AKMED

To Ali

So, what were you doing there, Ali?

ALI

I was running the bar, as usual.

AKMED

So, what was it like that day?

ALI

It was a Friday as I remember, so quite busy, that's when they had most of the popular crucifixions, there were a few Roman soldiers in the bar celebrating somebody's birthday, a few bank executives having a Friday afternoon piss up and an old Pharisee spouting off about the end of the world. It was pretty warm for Easter, as I remember.

AKMED

Akmed appears stunned by the detail

Warm for Easter? But surely that didn't start until/

ALI

Interrupts

/I picked up a nice bit of halibut for lunch, watched the crucifixion, then went back to work in the bar for the rest of the night, much the same as any other Friday in those days.

AKMED

Much the same as…. never mind,

Akmed turns back to Ali

what about the other one?

ALI

Other one, which other one?

AKMED

Muhammed, when he was killed.

ALI

Ah well, sort of self-inflicted that one. I remember it well. I'd been running my bar in a tiny Jewish settlement called Khaibar for about nine months, all very peaceful - they had a very lucrative Palm date business, very popular it was…

Anyway, Muhammed had a bit of a setback going to Mecca. Hence, as an act of contrition to Allah, he picked on Khaibar, as it was an easy target, lots of happy, inoffensive industrious Jewish families. He put most of them to the sword and appropriated the Palm date business.

Shamia looks on incredulously

Unfortunately, he became a little too friendly with one of the pretty Jewish girls just after the battle, perk of the job, you might say, and in return for services rendered, he promised not to chop her head off, so she cooked him and a few of his chums a lovely goat curry- she said it was lamb, but it wasn't, I knew the butcher - it was goat, anyway she poisoned the curry, and they all died, so that was that.

SHAMIA

That was that! Two prophets murdered, two sons of God zapped, and all you can say is, "that was that."

ALI

Well, it was, but of course, it didn't stop there. Been quite busy ever since, in fact. Always a bit of religious mayhem and slaughter going on somewhere. There's never a dull moment in conflict catering.

SHAMIA

You manage to get to most of the big shows, then?

ALI

I turn up whenever there's a bit of a do going on, yes. I hold my hands up to that. There's usually a big crowd. Hence, it's worth the effort, but only to sell some wine and a few nuts and olives, maybe the odd burger or Kebab, that's how I make a living.

CONT…

ALI

But I don’t do crucifixions anymore; it's all over too fast. Just the meaningless futile conflicts where there is never going to be a satisfactory outcome and where lots of people are involved; they tend to go on for years shooting the crap out of each other, gratuitous butchery can make you very thirsty, so its regular work and very remunerative.

SHAMIA

But why?

ALI

It’s what I do; as I said, it is regular work.

SHAMIA

But you’ve been turning up to these do’s for the best part of two thousand years doing this.

ALI

And?

SHAMIA

Well, don’t you ever get a bit tired of it all?

ALI

Not when you've got your hands on a nice little franchise like this. I'm tucking away quite a few bucks for my retirement, and it's better than running a Mucky D.

SHAMIA

Your retirement?

ALI

Not just yet, I got a few more years to go before then.

SHAMIA

Tell me this, how come you always know where to be?

ALI

I read the papers, watch a bit of telly, get the odd bit of inside information; that way, I usually turn up first and get the best spot.

SHAMIA

Inside information from who?

ALI

People who know people give me the nod when there's something significant about to kick off.

SHAMIA

Who exactly?

ALI

Well, I couldn't tell you that, could I? You might start up in competition. All you need to know is he knows what's going on and where and when; in fact, I wouldn't be surprised if he doesn't jolly them along a bit from time to time.

He taps the side of his nose.

SHAMIA

Its God!

ALI

Not quite, but you're getting warm.

He smirks to himself.

SHAMIA

Shamia looks confused.

But I'm a fanatical freedom fighter/

WALTER

/And a terrorist.

SHAMIA

Glares at Walter with contempt.

…and I ready to blow myself up for Allah, so I'm hardly going to open a quaint little chintzy wine bar just around the corner and steal all your punters, am I?

ALI

People change their career choice for all sorts of reasons, especially when push comes to shove. Look at you for instance, suddenly changed your mind about alcohol, and now you've developed an insatiable taste for Bacardi; You could be chucked out of the gang for that and beheaded,

He throws Ali an inquisitorial expression.

so, what next, I wonder…

SHAMIA

The drinking is all down to the stress. I get the twitches sometimes.

ALI

Is that why they call you…

SHAMIA

Reluctantly concedes the notion

Yes, I suppose so.

ALI

It could be a bit embarrassing if you had your finger on the trigger…

SHAMIA

Better keep me happy then, as I said, this is all very stressful.

ALI

Maybe, but it does show you that people do change their minds under the right circumstances.

SHAMIA

But I'm a dedicated Freedom fighter/

WALTER

Interrupts

/And a terrorist.

Shamia sneers at Walter and mimics a flat hand throat-cutting gesture.

ALI

Maybe, but as I said, even you might suddenly have a change of heart, decide to relinquish your suicidal quest to destroy all infidels in the world and open a wine bar or a Persian restaurant in Bognor Regis.

WALTER

Your mum does run a Kebab takeaway.

SHAMIA

That's got nothing to do with me.

ALI

Easy for you to say, but you've got doner in the blood.

AKMED

It kind of throws a slightly different light on Mr Hitler though, maybe he was just implementing appropriate retribution on behalf of Christians and Muslims for what the Jews did to Jesus and Mohammed?

Everybody looks at Akmed, who has just woken up.

ALI AND SHAMIA

What?

AKMED

Just now, you were talking about the Jews taking out Jesus and Allah.

ALI

I thought you were asleep.

AKMED

Meditating.

Ali shrugs

WALTER

I hardly think frying six million Jews was an equitable justification for the unsubstantiated and slightly contentious death of two slightly dubious Prophets.

SHAMIA

Allah is not a dubious prophet.

Waves a finger at Ali admonishingly

WALTER

I thought Allah was born clutching an AK47.

SHAMIA

That is a blasphemous caricature created by the American infidels at the CIA to distort the perceived image of Allah. At this rate, you could very quickly be nominated for a second fatwa.

WALTER

Walter starts shaking his hands and making a funny expression as if petrified with fear.

Look at me; I'm pissing myself.

SHAMIA

They will cut your head off to stop you from uttering these sacrilegious profanities.

WALTER

Well, at least I wouldn't have to listen to your crazy ramblings anymore, and how exactly are you going to chop my head off twice?

SHAMIA

Shamia is beginning to rage with frustration

Your soul will never sleep for saying these accursed things!

WALTER

Not a problem, I don't have one. I sold it years ago.

SHAMIA

Shamia looks astounded

You can't sell your soul.

WALTER

Of course, you can. Anybody can if you want to pay the price.

SHAMIA

I don't believe you - you are mad. This is typical Yankee propaganda - you can't sell your soul.

WALTER

Now come on, Shaky, you know it's true. Everybody knows that.

Dizzie, JJ, Ali acknowledge what Walter has said.

SHAMIA

Don't call me Shaky my name is Shamia.

WALTER

Getting a bit touchy, are we?

SHAMIA

No.

WALTER

Looks like you are to me; I saw your finger inching towards the trigger.

SHAMIA

It was not.

ALI

Your gun won't work in here, Shaky. You should know that.

SHAMIA

What do you mean it won't work?

ALI

The bar is a partially exempt area from hostile activities it's in the lease.

SHAMIA

Partially exempt? What shit is that?

ALI

Exactly what I said.

SHAMIA

I don't understand.

ALI

I've told you before Shaky, I sold my soul to the Redemptor years ago, so I can't be killed, and neither can anybody else while they are in here. You just never believe me.

SHAMIA

You are taking the piss. There's no such person as the Redemptor.

ALI

Oh, but there is, but don't take my word for it, try it if you like, believe me, it won't work.

SHAMIA

Shamia points his gun at the ceiling and pulls the trigger. It makes an ineffectual farting noise but nothing else,

What have you done to my gun? You've made me bloody impotent. I'm like a man without a dick.

Shamia expresses indignation.

The ensemble is laughing.

ALI

Well, I wouldn't go quite that far, just fun-loving, amiable, and ineffectual – maybe even a little bit chilled, once you settle down and accept the situation.

SHAMIA

That's the same thing. What fucking use is a suicidal freedom fighter whose gun doesn't work and who has suddenly become fun-loving and amiable.

WALTER

And a terrorist.

SHAMIA

Reluctantly and with another sneer at Walter

And terrorist.

ALI

It will work outside the bar, just not in here, so you can play with your weapon all you like when you get outside.

SHAMIA

Thank you, what about the Semtex.

ALI

Don't pull the trigger on that!

Ali appears alarmed. Dizzie starts filming Shamia.

SHAMIA

Ah, I have got you all now.

WHOLE CAST

No, don't pull the fucking trigger!!

SHAMIA

Shamia pulls a ripcord by his side, and a cloud of flour and sparkly glitter explodes in the air and completely covers him. He screams...

Ahhhhhh, what is all this shit?

ALI

We did warn you.

Shamia, now covered in flour and sparkling glitter, is extremely unhappy. He tries to say something, but nothing can be heard above the laughing.

DIZZIE

Dizzie has been filming Shamia.

Hey, I got some great footage. I can "bang" that straight onto YouTube that is just going to go so seriously viral. Your mates will love it Shaky.

SHAMIA

Oh, for Christ's sake, please don't do that. My image and credibility as a freedom fighter will be blown to pieces.

A few more giggles from the cast.

DIZZIE

Very good.

Shamia has missed the pun.

WALTER

And a terrorist.

SHAMIA

Sharply

And a bloody terrorist.

DIZZIE

Oh, and who's name did you just take in vain?

SHAMIA

I meant for Allah's sake, not Christ's.

DIZZIE

Can you take Allah's name in vain?

SHAMIA

Well, no, it's punishable by death.

DIZZIE

Oops, another cockup. That's another fatwa.

He makes a clownlike facial expression dropping one side of his bottom lip

SHAMIA

Shamia flops down on a barstool

This is really pissing me off. First, it's new bar rules, then my gun stops working, and now I'm covered in sparkly shit, and I can't self-explode. I'm beginning to feel very depressed.... another Coke, please, Ali.

ALI

Neat?

SHAMIA

Maybe a smidgen of Bacardi

Ali feels the glass with Bacardi and puts in a tiny splash of coke

Thank you.

Shamia takes a huge gulp.

WALTER

Stress can give you high blood pressure Shaky.

SHAMIA

What?

WALTER

Hypertension, you should keep an eye on that. It can be a killer.

SHAMIA looks concerned

ALI

So how is your blood pressure? Has your doctor checked you out recently?

SHAMIA

It's a little high, but the doc's put me on...

(He pulls out a strip of pills from a pocket and reads)

Bendroflumethiazide, he says that if I keep taking the pills and avoid unnecessary stress, I could easily live till I'm eighty, so it's okay.

CAST

Everybody looks at Shamia, appearing a little stunned by his statement.

ALI

Eighty?

SHAMIA

He looks surprised by Ali's exclamation.

Yes, no problem. Why?

WALTER

I wonder if having your body shot full of bullet holes lowers your blood pressure?

The whole cast looks across at Walter in disbelief at his comment.

JJ

JJ looks confused.

Isn't that a bit…. (*He stops*)

SHAMIA

Thanks for asking Ali. It's nice to know someone cares.

ALI

No problem, I like to take an interest in my customer's health and welfare; it's part of my ongoing care in the community policy.

WALTER

It can be a real bummer high blood pressure, stress management that's what you need.

SHAMIA

Stress management?

WALTER

That's the secret. You must learn to manage pressure. Avoid stressful situations, think pleasant thoughts, and don't do anything too erratic. Try a little yoga from time to time; that's what I do.

SHAMIA

Yoga?

Shamia appears confused

MORGIANA

Whale music.

SHAMIA

What?

MORGIANA

Whale music, you should try listening to that on your Ipod whenever you have the opportunity.

DIZZIE

Like in between firefights and mortar attacks, you mean?

MORGIANA

Any time's good.

DIZZIE

I can just picture it now… gunfire from all directions, shells exploding everywhere, occasional rocket strike from above and Shaky swaying gently to the harmonious sounds of humping whales.

MORGIANA

Morgiana waves her cocktail glass at Ali

Another Strawberry Daiquiri, Ali. Please.

Morgiana, now a little drunk, turns to Dizzie.

I was only trying to help.

DIZZIE

Dizzie throws his hands up in a gesture of understanding

SHAMIA

I didn't know you had high blood pressure Walter.

WALTER

You never asked. I've had it for years.

SHAMIA

So, what causes it?

WALTER

Anything… even having a quiet drink is becoming stressful these days…

Shamia is still dusting off some of the flour and sparkle.

SHAMIA

I've never seen you do anything stressful.

WALTER

I try not to, it's not a problem. You just have to take it steady, chill and try not to get too wired. Sometimes though, stress can creep up on you unawares.

SHAMIA

Can it?

DIZZIE

Like when there's a rocket attack?

WALTER

Yea, that could do it.

SHAMIA

Well, I'm sorry for getting a bit loud just now. I didn't realise.

WALTER

Me too. I shouldn't have picked on you. It's not your fault; in fact, it was pretty amusing for five minutes, which always helps to relieve the tension - a laugh and a joke.

SHAMIA

Does it?

WALTER

Oh yes, absolutely.

SHAMIA

Being here must be a bit stressful, though?

WALTER

No worse than being home with the wife and kids.

SHAMIA

Long pause………

So, Ali, when did the new rules start?

ALI

Three weeks ago.

SHAMIA

Three weeks ago! But I haven't been here for three weeks.

ALI

No, you haven't.

SHAMIA

It's not very democratic implementing new rules without consulting all interested parties.

ALI

We thought you were dead.

SHAMIA

Oh, that's charming. I can't get in for three weeks because I'm otherwise engaged, so you assume I'm dead and take the opportunity to implement new house rules. Some sort of egalitarian fraternity this is. I bet you had a little party as well... didn't you?

MORGIANA

Just a few drinks to celebrate your life and death, nothing to elaborate, we thought that…

Morgiana waves her cocktail at Shamia

SHAMIA

Well, that was nice.

MORGIANA

We enjoyed it.

JJ

We must have rules. If we didn't, everything would quickly descend into chaos and anarchy, and anarchy leads to revolution.

AKMED

Akmed has fallen asleep at the bar again but suddenly wakes.

Viva, the revolution!

JJ

What!

AKMED

Somebody said revolution!

JJ

I just said that… oh forget it.

Akmed goes back to sleep.

SHAMIA

Anarchy and chaos?

Shamia appears stunned

Have you been outside recently?

JJ

Absolutely not. I don't like loud noises or surprises much… unless it's someone buying me a drink.

He looks around the bar, but nobody responds.

AKMED

Wakes up momentarily again.

I'm perfectly happy with the rules. I've never blown myself up in here, have I? and why?... because it's a rule.

(Akmed points to the sign behind the bar)

NO SELF EXPLODING FREEDOM FIGHTERS ADMITTED, AND NO LOUD OR OFFENSIVE POLITICAL RHETORIC ALLOWED AT ANY TIME.

DIZZIE

Ah, but you tried…

Directed at SHAMIA

SHAMIA

You provoked me. And anyway, that doesn't count as it didn't work, and I am still here… in one piece.

Dizzie flashes Shamia a withering glare.

DIZZIE

Fortunately.

Still flicking glitter off his jacket.

ALI

So, Shaky, where have you been. You are obviously not dead?

SHAMIA

The wife has been having pottery lessons in the evenings, so she made me stay in and look after baby Abdullah.

WALTER

Say, how is the little guy? He must be what, nearly three now?

SHAMIA

He's four in June, and he's just fine. He stripped down and reassembled his own AK47 yesterday for the first time without any help. We are all very proud of him. We bought it as an early Christmas present. He, too, will grow up and one day become a great freedom fighter.

WALTER

Or a terrorist?

SHAMIA

Shamia gives Walter another withering glance

JJ

But you don't celebrate the birth of Jesus!

SHAMIA

No, not as such, but I try to stay open-minded and nonpartisan, not too radicalised. We are learning to embrace and tolerate most religions. I like that pudding thing with all the fruit; Shakira always makes me one every year. And of course, I like pulling the crackers…
BANG!

Shamia shouts the word, throws his arms out and everybody jumps. He smiles with a demented expression.

JJ

That's not very funny.

SHAMIA

SHAMIA feigns an apologetic expression

It's great fun, though.

WALTER

We really did think you were dead. You kept talking about all those virgins, so we sort of assumed that…you know you'd done the firecracker thing.

Walter wiggles two fingers on each hand

It's only now, seeing everything's still "Intact," so to speak, if you know what I mean and that you are okay that we…

SHAMIA

Subhanallah!

Shamia throws his arms into the air

You shouldn't just assume things. I will let you know when I'm not coming back. But at the moment, I am still waiting for the call. So, I'm okay, but my life is still dedicated to Allah, and one day I will die a glorious death and be remembered as a great freedom fighter.

WALTER

Or…/

SHAMIA

Shamia quickly interrupts.

/Freedom fighter!

WALTER

Freedom from what, though.

SHAMIA

Tyranny and oppression.

WALTER

By whom?

SHAMIA

Anyone who happens to be here, Americans, English, Christian, Jews, Sunni's, Kurds, Russians.

Akmed flashes a surprised expression, but Shamia waves his hand in a gesture to indicate that his brother is not included.

WALTER

So how do you intend to fight this tyranny and oppression?

SHAMIA

By terrorising everybody, then killing them.

WALTER

So, you are a terrorist?

SHAMIA

No freedom fighter.

WALTER

So let me get this right, you are a freedom fighter who uses tyranny and oppression to defeat a freely elected government now run by tyrants and oppressors. Then you select yourself as the new government now made up of ex-freedom fighters who become the new tyrants and oppressors using tyranny and oppression to rule the country.

SHAMIA

That about sums it up, I think.

WALTER

So, what's the difference?

SHAMIA

Difference?

WALTER

Between a terrorist and a freedom fighter.

SHAMIA

Nothing really. But freedom fighter is so much catchier media-wise. It conjures up the vision of a romanticised iconic hero.

Shamia looks skywards wistfully and adopts a ridiculous pose with both arms raised to the heavens.

MORGIANA

Or a heroine. Don't forget women. We can be enigmatic and charismatic too.

Everybody looks at Morgiana in amazement.
The room goes silent for a moment as everybody inwardly digests Morgiana's declaration.

SHAMIA

I don't think so. Women have no position in our society. They make babies, clean the house, cook food and operate the washing machine; that's it.

Dizzie, JJ, Walter, Ali and Morgiana stare at Shamia in amazement

MORGIANA

And that's how Shakira sees it?

SHAMIA

Yes!... more or less.
The last three words are mumbled.

MORGIANA

I think less, a lot less.

ALI

So, you see yourself as a bit of a Che Guevara?

SHAMIA AND AKMED

A mantra

"Hail Che, the immortal hero of all Freedom Fighters"

Ali points to the sign about Rhetoric.

Shamia and Akmed both nod their heads contritely.

SHAMIA

Your lot started it.

Shamia points at Walter.

WALTER

Don't blame me. I'm just working for CNN.

SHAMIA

Well, obviously not you personally, but you do represent the Infidels of America, and they did invade and infiltrate our country.

WALTER

Now steady on there. Firstly, I do not represent my country. I am just here to report the news in an unbiased and non-partisan manner without any political, religious, ethnic or moral bias. I could be from anywhere. And secondly, more importantly, as I see it, your lot did make a formal request for us to invade.

SHAMIA

My Lot?

WALTER

Well, no, Akmed's, actually.

AKMED

Shamia glances at Akmed

We had a bit of a problem with some Kurds that were being troublesome. So, yes. We did borrow a few bits and bobs from the Americans.

WALTER

Astonishment

Bits and bobs?

AKMED

Indignantly

Yes.

WALTER

The last I heard it was two armoured divisions, three ground force battalions, and three aircraft squadrons – one special op's brigade and a satellite ground observation facility. That's not exactly what I call a *few bits and bobs.*

AKMED

It seemed like a good idea at the time.

SHAMIA
To kill a few Sunni Kurds?

AKMED
More or less.

WALTER
But you're a Sunni Muslim.

AKMED
A Sunni Arab, not a Sunni Kurd, there is a distinction.

WALTER
Is there? I can't see it.

AKMED
It's complex,

WALTER
I can see that.

AKMED
Shall I try to explain?

WALTER
Please do.

AKMED

Well, you see, the Sunni Kurds were becoming a real pain in the arse.
The Turks were bombing them from one direction with equipment supplied by Russia, and to help out, Saddam and his crew started bombing and gassing them from the other direction with more equipment provided by/

ALI

/Don't tell me the Americans.

AKMED

Bang on. However, once Saddam gassed the Kurds, who were, coincidently, his own people - the ones he didn't manage to kill became a bit upset. When they complained about the atrocity, it attracted some attention.

WALTER

From whom?

AKMED

Just about everybody, but particularly the Americans, because it was against international law to gas people.

CONT

AKMED CONT…

The Americans didn't mind Saddam killing his own people nicely but gassing them was definitely not on. It sends out the wrong message and creates a lot of media attention. So, a lot of people got upset… a bit.

WALTER

Not to mention a few Kurds.

AKMED

A few.

ALI

But didn't the Americans supply Saddam with the gas in the first place?

AKMED

Ah, now you're beginning to understand the irony and the paradox.

WALTER

So, we were sort of invited to come in and put a stop to Saddam's nastiness.

SHAMIA

So, you did invade us.

WALTER

The US of A came in by invitation, not me personally. I came much later, by coach.

SHAMIA

By bloody invitation? It wasn't a Bar Mitzvah. I wasn't aware we sent out RSVP invites to invade.

WALTER

Well, somebody did.

SHAMIA

Who? It wasn't us?

WALTER

The Kurds.

SHAMIA

The Kurds, so the Russians supply weapons to the Turks. The UK and the USA provided weapons to Saddam to kill Kurds and Iranians, and when the Kurds complain about it, you come straight in and decimate our peaceful country and turn on Saddam.

WALTER

Well, it was hardly peaceful, was it.

Pause then sound of gunshots and explosions

SHAMIA

Not now, no.

WALTER

As I remember, Old Saddam once gassed a complete Kurdish village because they forgot to celebrate his fiftieth birthday.

SHAMIA

He was bereft at the oversite and was having a bad day.

WALTER

Not as bad as the Kurds.

SHAMIA

The Kurds are always whinging about something.

WALTER

It wasn't just the Kurds; your lot were complaining as well.

SHAMIA

Our lot? by that, I presume you are referring to the indigenous people of Iraq?

WALTER

Not Specifically? I believe it was the Sunni crowd who first complained.

SHAMIA

Oh, so it's Akmed's fault now, is it?

AKMED

Don't drag me into this, Bro? I'm just trying to have a quiet drink. I never complained about anything.

WALTER

You're already in it up to your ……. Ears

AKMED

AKMED is combing his hair and gazing into a hand mirror he has produced from somewhere. He turns to Walter.

Tell me something, Walter?

WALTER

Yes, Akmed.

AKMED

Do you think I look a little like Brad Pitt?

WALTER

What?

AKMED

Brad Pitt, American actor.

WALTER

The question confounds Walter.

Yes, I know who you mean, but no, you don't, not in the slightest.

Akmed takes no notice of Walter's repudiation and continues to preen himself.

AKMED

Are you sure?

WALTER

Positive.

AKMED

Akmed pauses for a few moments.

George Clooney, then?

WALTER

Nope.

AKMED

Fair enough, but I think you're gravely mistaken.

He puts the mirror away.

SHAMIA

Slowly with a philosophical inclination, Shamia speaks to Walter.

Tell me something, if we'd never had any oil.... would you have bothered to invade?

WALTER

I don't know because I didn't invade, but to answer, on behalf of the American people, I believe they came to save you from Saddam the Stalinist oppressor and his despotic, dictatorial regime and to "wipe those baddies from the face of the earth" to quote Ronald Reagan/

ALI

Abruptly intervening and pointing at the "No Rhetoric" sign,

/Rules!! Getting a little contentious there, Walter.

WALTER

Sorry, Ali, I'll rephrase… to help you reconfigure a constitutional voting system and facilitate a democratically elected government?

ALI

Better.

WALTER

No problem.

Directed to Shamia

And to answer your question, Shaky, of course, we would.

CONT....

WALTER CONT…

The oil's not important; we just want the whole world to enjoy the same sort of progressive liberal-centric, peace-loving democracy that we do.

AKMED

Whether they want it or not.

WALTER

Sometimes, people don't really know what they want, so it becomes necessary to point them in the right direction and help them see things from a different perspective, occasionally with a tangible tactical aid to assist in the formation of a democracy

AKMED

What's a tangible tactical aid?

WALTER

It's sort of like an invasion.

AKMED

Invasion!

WALTER

Yes, but with technical consultants and advisors.

AKMED

That's not a democracy. That's just another covert fascist dictatorship.

ALI

Rules…. sorry, lads.

Akmed and Walter mumble incoherently

AKMED

But what if we had no oil like shaky suggested.

WALTER

No oil?

AKMED

None

WALTER

And no other mineral resources?

AKMED

Nothing except sand and a few camels.

WALTER

Well, probably not. There's a lot of other countries that need our help in forming a transparent and accountable regi… ah, sorry, government.

AKMED

Whether they like it or not?

WALTER
Possibly…. Sometimes, but that's because many countries haven't benefited from our vast experience solving world problems.

Spasmodic external shooting increases in intensity.

AKMED
What and you really believe you do?

WALTER
We are an old and wise country and have been involved in many direct and indirect tactical struggles over the last hundred years. So, we have acquired considerable personal experience to which we can refer.

AKMED
Mainly wars and invasions, as I recall.

WALTER
Occasionally invasion is a necessary evil.

AKMED
Nearly always from what I've seen.

WALTER

When there's a little bit of local difficulty, we usually find it easier to help sort things out by having a physical presence on the ground. People find that a calming and reassuring influence.

Akmed looks stunned. His mouth falls open.

AKMED

Like Korea, Vietnam, Beirut, Afghanistan, Ireland and about two hundred other conflicts started by the US of A, in fact, out of 248 armed conflicts worldwide since 1945, the good old US of A started 201 of them.

WALTER

No, not Ireland. We've never started anything there.

AKMED

No, that one was a little different. You were just arming the terrorists who were fighting the British.

WALTER

That was never proved.

Akmed gives Walter a sceptical glare.

SHAMIA

There's no oil there either, just a peat bog and some lucky gipsy heather. There's not much you can do with that.

WALTER

America unfailingly achieves a result.

AKMED

Well, surely that depends on how you define the result.

DIZZIE

Reading from his laptop.

A result is the final consequence of a sequence of actions or events expressed qualitatively or quantitatively. Possible results include advantage, disadvantage, gain, injury, loss, value and victory.

Dizzie glances up and smiles

SHAMIA

What about a disastrous and catastrophic withdrawer? Isn't that included?

DIZZIE

No.

AKMED
How many conflicts have you actually won?

WALTER
Well, that depends on how you want to define winning.

AKMED
Here we go again, juggling the words to make them fit the question. I thought there was only one way to define the winner…. One side gives up, and the other takes everything! And everybody is happy as lamb afterwards - spending their weekends dancing round maypoles merrily singing cheery little ditties… So, tell me, how many times has that happened?

WALTER
Well, not that many, I grant you. Not using that sort of disingenuous and highly unfavourable analogy. I suppose from time to time, the outcome can be a little misunderstood and misconstrued.

AKMED
Misconstrued! Holy Jesus, we wouldn't want that to happen, would we?

WALTER

It is a complex and emotive subject; we can't possibly know or understand all the intangibles and unknowns… What appears to be a disaster one day may not actually be a disaster after all. Not when you look back at it a few years later. Time does lend a certain enchantment.

AKMED

Nothing is enchanting about serial invasion. This is not rocket science - it's plain simple maths. Oh, and by the way, I haven't included another couple of hundred conflicts which the US of A was involved in covertly, so we're talking about over four hundred wars, invasions, mini-invasions, contretemps and minor tactical disagreements over nearly sixty-five years, that's some achievement.

WALTER

We're getting better at it.

AKMED

Are you, are you really? I think America is like the petroleum it so much adores.

WALTER

Petrol? I don't understand.

AKMED

Everybody needs it, but it will explode in your face if you are careless when it's around. Nobody should invite America to dinner. They eat everything.

SHAMIA

If they were a football team, we would have shot the manager by now.

DIZZIE

So, would we…

Realizes what he has said.

Or maybe not.

Walter, Shamia, and Ali glance at Dizzie puzzlingly

SHAMIA

So, you agree?

WALTER

What?

SHAMIA

That it's a bit of a cock-up here?

WALTER

Not at all.

SHAMIA

What do you need to be convinced? Everybody dead?

WALTER

America will sort this war out eventually.

SHAMIA

That's very comforting, but how exactly do they fix this?

The centre doors swing open, and Dave strolls in. He is wearing a large white cloak with ornate black trimming. He speaks with a London accent. The sound of gunshots, explosions can be heard.

DAVE

Brightly

Yo people.

ALI

Welcome friend.

WALTER

Hi.

SHAMIA

Wa Alaykum s-salaam

Morgiana waves her glass. Dizzie and JJ hold up their drinks. Akmed does nothing.

ALI

Can I get you something?

DAVE

What do you recommend?

ALI

Beers good.

DAVE

I'll have a beer then, thanks.

ALI

Cold beer coming up.

DAVE

Looks slowly around the bar at the customers.

ALI

We don't see many strangers in here.

Increased external shooting, shouting and screaming, and explosions can be heard.

DAVE

No, I don't suppose you do, not with all that going on.

Dave sips his beer and slowly raises his hand up.

ALI

I'm sorry about the noise but...

At that precise moment, Dave waves his hand and the shooting stops.

Dave continues drinking his beer.

CAST

Everybody in the bar stops what they are doing and look around at each other - a little surprised by the sudden cessation of external battle sounds.

DAVE

Problem?

ALI

Not at all, it's just that… the racket seldom stops in the evening…. Not until…

DAVE

Well, that's good innit?

ALI

Yes, that's good… by the way - I didn't mention it when you first came in but, we have a few house rules you should know about if that is okay with you? Makes it a friendlier little bar.

Ali points to all the signs.

Dave looks around the bar at all the signs and slowly scans all the drinkers.

DAVE

Yes, I know, that's why I came.

ALI

Right.

Ali looks at Dave curiously

AKMED

So, you here on business?

DAVE

Sort of, I'm into reclamation, recovery, retrieval and redemption.

AKMED

Smiles.

You're a scrap metal dealer.

DAVE

No, I tend to major in the redemption aspect.

AKMED

Well, you've come to the right place for that, anything in particular?

DAVE

Carpets, rare carpets to be precise, but I also do a little part-time work in perdition.

WALTER

Walter turns to Morgiana

Doesn't your husband sell carpets?

MORGIANA

Yep! The good for nothing lecherous bastard does, occasionally, when he's sober. But he spends most of his time screwing whores on the stock.

Morgiana is still a little drunk.

ALI

Walter turns back to Dave

You wouldn't have thought there was much demand for carpets out here… right now, what with/

MORGIANA

Interrupts

/That's what I told the stupid bastard before we came here. And if you take my advice, mister, you wanner jump straight back on your carpet and f.. f.. f.. fly off somewhere nicer than this f.f.. f.f... Godforsaken shithole because you won't sell any bloody carpets, and as sure as hell, you'll probably get your arse shot off.

DAVE

Thanks, I'll remember that.

He holds his glass up to Morgiana to say thanks.

MORGIANA

Morgiana mumbles something incoherent.

AKMED

Take no notice; she's just a little tired and emotional.

DAVE

Understandable.

WALTER

So, are you going to be around for a while?

DAVE

I don't know. It depends.

WALTER

What, whether you sell some carpets.

DAVE

Well, no, I don't actually sell carpets; I just collect valuable ones and sometimes trade them. It's just a hobby, you understand.

Dave finishes his beer.

ALI

A hobby I see…… another beer… on the house?

DAVE

That's very hospitable; yes, yes I will, thanks.

ALI

I didn't think we had any rare carpets around here. Nearly everything has been burnt, looted or is being used to block a hole in something.

DAVE

Well, it wasn't just the carpets, I'm on holiday as well.

ALI

You're on holiday... a sort of Iraqi mini break is it.?

DAVE

Yea, something like that.

ALI

Bit hairy going on holiday in a major war zone. Thomas Cook cheapy was it? Off the internet?

DAVE

I like the unusual, and I enjoy finding a new challenge each day.

ALI

Well, this is unusual, and it's definitely a challenge every day here… just staying alive.

Ali starts to hum Staying Alive by the Bee Gee's

DAVE

You don't appear overly concerned about what's going on?

ALI

I live here, it's an old established family business, and I don't have anywhere else to go at the moment.

DAVE

No…what I meant was how come you're still running a bar in the middle of a war zone when everybody else has gone?

Dave flashes Ali a conspiratorial expression.

ALI

Smiles… he has realised something

A bit like you, in a way, I like a challenge, and I do have my regulars to look after…

He waves his open palms to everybody.

They all smile back.

…and the odd passing stranger.

Ali points a finger at Dave.

Dave smiles

MORGIANA

Morgiana interrupts.

My husband's still here with his bloody carpet shop.

Morgiana slides off her barstool and wanders over to a small round table with her cocktail glass in hand. She sits down.

ALI

Somebody's got to do it.

DAVE

But this is a dangerous place to be right now?

ALI

It's relative.

DAVE

To what?

ALI

What you consider dangerous, I mean you're here on holiday, so it can't be too bad.

DAVE

But this must be one of the most perilous places on earth right now.

ALI

Not really.

DAVE

What do you mean not really? What about the shooting and constant airstrikes?

There is still silence.

ALI

I can't hear anything right now… which is a little unusual, I will admit.

Dave flashes his hand
The external noise recommences

DAVE

What that!

ALI

It was okay just now.

DAVE

Well, it's not now, is it?

ALI

You get used to it.

DAVE

So why aren't they fighting?

He gestures across to Akmed and Shamia, who are whispering to each other.

ALI

What Akmed and Shamia?

DAVE

Yes, they are Shi'ite and Sunni, aren't they?

ALI

That's what the badges say.

DAVE

Then, why aren't they?

ALI

Two reasons.

DAVE

Yes.

ALI

Well firstly the rules, that's the most important reason,

Ali points to the rules,

and then…. they are brothers

DAVE

We're all brothers.

ALI

No, they really are brothers.

DAVE

But aren't they on different sides?

ALI

In a manner of speaking, they are.

DAVE

What does that mean?

ALI

Well, they are not actually on different sides; that's a popular misconception. More like both sides of the same coin, if you see what I mean.

They're both Muslims; it's just a difference of opinion on their interpretation of history. The real problem here is the Americans are backing one lot and not the other, so they are surreptitiously inciting a religious civil war.

The Russians are supporting the other side as they too, would like to gain access to the historical culture and heritage of the country… and the oil…

The only real difference is who has the biggest guns. The Russians and The Americans are both hoping the locals will kill each other in their entirety, then they can drive in when it all goes quiet and take control of all the oil wells.

CONT…

ALI CONT…

The Musi's aren't a bad lot once you get to know them. Kick the invaders out, ban religion, and it would be like Disney Land, but that will never happen. And anyway, that would be bad for my business if worldwide peace suddenly broke out.

DAVE

Intriguing.

ALI

Why?

DAVE

You appeared to have defined the problem and proposed a solution in little more than a blink of an eye.

ALI

Maybe, maybe not, but does it help? I don't think so.

DAVE

Well, it helps to keep the peace in here.

ALI

No, that's the rules. Nobody wants to be barred.

DAVE

Barred, how could you bar anybody?

ALI

I just tell them they can't come back.

DAVE

And they would accept that?

ALI

Well, I hope so, but it's never been tested, no need, you see everybody abides by…

DAVE

The rules.

ALI

Exactly. And one of the rules is no arguing with the landlord.

Ali points to another sign

DAVE

I am beginning to think there's more to you than meets the eye. You're not just a humble innkeeper, are you?

ALI

Ali smiles and continues polishing a glass.

Well, you're a pretty mysterious person yourself. That little trick with your fingers was very impressive.

DAVE

Oh, you noticed that?

ALI

Yes.

DAVE

Conjurers' misdirection and prestidigitation, it's all in the fingers.

Rolls his fingers

ALI

Is it?

With a nuance of disbelief

DAVE

Dave nods and strolls slowly over to where Morgiana is now sitting. Flamboyantly swishing his cloak as he goes. All the lights fade down to just a spotlight over Morgiana and Dave.

MORGIANA

I do love your cloak.

DAVE

Pauses before answering what is obviously a well-rehearsed reply.

And I… love your eyes

MORGIANA

Are you hitting on me?

DAVE

Nope, just complimenting your eyes. Why should I be hitting on you?

MORGIANA

I don't know; it just sounded….

DAVE

Morgiana, isn't it?

MORGIANA

Yes. But you can call me Max; Morgiana's a bit of a mouthful.

DAVE

It's a pretty mouth.

The ensemble makes throwing up gestures, noises and comments. "For fuck's sake get a room, get a bucket etc."

MORGIANA

Morgiana smiles.

Now that was… Seriously cheesy, but I liked it.

DAVE

Max, would you like another drink?

MORGIANA

Is Pinocchio a Catholic?

DAVE

confused

What?

MORGIANA

Sorry, I fucked that up a little; what I meant to say was - does the Pope have wooden balls?

DAVE

Still confused but smiles anyway.

I'll take that as a yes.

MORGIANA

Morgiana smiles and finishes off her cocktail and puts the glass in front of Dave.

DAVE

What is it?

MORGIANA

It's a Hammer.

DAVE

Which is what?

MORGIANA

Three shots of Vodka, one Gherkin, a splash of Cinzano, another shot of Vodka and a hint of Jack and coke.

DAVE.

Right

He gestures across to Ali for another cocktail

Do you mind if I sit down... Max?

MORGIANA

Not my chairs, and my husband hasn't turned up yet, so…

DAVE

I'll take that as a yes?

He sits.

MORGIANA

So why are you here, Dave?

She overemphasises "Dave."

DAVE

I'm in carpets; I collect rare ones. Didn't I mention that earlier? Same as your husband, I believe?

MORGIANA

Ex at the rate we're going.

DAVE

I'm sorry.

MORGIANA

Nothing to be sorry about; he's a bum.

DAVE

But you still love him?

MORGIANA

Loving him and living with him are two very different arrangements.

DAVE

So, what are you going to do?

MORGIANA

I haven't made my mind up yet, but I might leave and then I might not.

DAVE

What are you going to do if you leave?

MORGIANA

Go back home - be an actress.

DAVE

An actress?

MORGIANA

I was in Star Wars, very small part. I was this weird looking tart with three tits.

DAVE

I don't remember the character.

MORGIANA

You wouldn't, it was a very small part, she also had two heads, but they were both ugly.

DAVE

Emm…

MORGIANA

So why are you here, really? I might be a bit pissed, but I'm not stupid.

DAVE

I didn't think you were.

MORGIANA

You didn't have to be?

DAVE

What do you mean?

MORGIANA

I don't think you collect rare carpets. All the good ones were stolen by the Americans on day one. You would know that, and anyway, you don't look the carpet collector type. I don't think you're a holidaymaker on a day trip from Bagdad either.

DAVE

I didn't say Bagdad.

MORGIANA

You know what I mean. You might be able to fool this lot of cretins, but I've been around a bit, and there's something about you, something I can't quite put my finger on… but I will…

DAVE

You're very perceptive Max, and there's a subtle, understated astuteness in what you say, but/

MORGIANA

/Now you're patronising me because I'm very drunk, and that's taking an unfair advantage.

DAVE

What if I told you I could give you anything you wanted?

Morgiana smiles, feigning coquettishness.

MORGIANA

If you want to fuck me, just ask? You don't have to piss around with all the Moon and the stars bullshit. I've had all that "I'm goner make you are star crap" before - I'm immune to it now.

DAVE

Yes, I thought you would be. Look, I don't want to fuck you, as you so nicely put it, well actually I wouldn't mind, but not right now, and thanks for the offer, by the way, that was very generous. But I do have a few other things that need to be sorted out first.

MORGIANA

Slightly disappointed.

I see.

DAVE

I am visiting… but I live a little further away than Bagdad.

MORGIANA

I bet you're from a parallel universe where everybody's dreams come true?

Morgiana glances slowly around the room.

DAVE

Who are you looking for?

MORGIANA

Not who, what. I'm looking for the portal to this other world.

DAVE

Smiles

There you go again, nonchalant yet astute with your perception, it's not quite that, but you're definitely in the right area.

MORGIANA

Right... and what's going on in this other world?

DAVE

Well, much the same as here except for some of the bad bits.

MORGIANA

No arsehole husbands, then?

DAVE

Sorry, we still have those.

MORGIANA

Are shoes free?

With a smile

DAVE

Sorry, no free shoes.

MORGIANA

It doesn't sound much better than here as far as I can make out. Are you sure you're not just a little bit drunker than me?

DAVE

I'm not drunk.

MORGIANA

No, you're not, are you? So, what's it got, this other world? Don't tell me… pretty two-headed women, with three tits?

DAVE

No, we're all normal, more or less.

MORGIANA

So, what is this "anything" that you can give me?

DAVE

I'll tell you later… if you are interested.

The lights go up on the set.
Dave smiles and walks to the other end of the bar where Shamia and Akmed are talking. Dizzie, JJ and Walter are huddled around a table, talking quietly.
Morgiana gets up and walks back to her place at the end of the bar.

DAVE

Do you mind if I join you?

SHAMIA

Not at all.

DAVE

So, you two are both… freedom fighters, I understand?

AKMED

We are.

WALTER

Shouts

Terrorists.

AKMED

Take no notice; he's American. They despise everybody. If they don't understand something, they either invade it or fuck it.

DAVE

So, it wouldn't be unreasonable for me to hazard a guess that your life expectancy is, how shall I put this without being too indelicate… edging towards the shorter end of… brief?

AKMED
Compact and fulfilled with accomplishments is how I like to think of it. Time is relative to how you fill it. A life full of achievements or full of nothing, that's the choice.

DAVE
But still a bit short?

SHAMIA
If we die, we go to a better world, and if that is the will of Allah, so be it.

DAVE
But you could have the best of both worlds.

AKMED
How?

DAVE
You could trade something you have for something I want.

AKMED
We've got nothing to trade except sand.

DAVE
I am sure I could find something more valuable.

SHAMIA

And what would we get in return for this valuable something?

DAVE

Whatever you want, but it's usually time. I can throw in a few other benefits if you like.

AKMED

What do you mean, time?

DAVE

Just that. Is that so hard to understand?

AKMED

Sounds too good to be true and in my experience.../

DAVE

/Look, you don't have to take my word for it, but the question you should ask yourself is what have you got to lose?

SHAMIA

Well, I don't know, it depends on what you want.

DAVE

I promise you, you can afford it, and it won't really cost you anything in the end.

SHAMIA

So, we can have whatever we want, virtually for nothing. Is that it?

DAVE

Not quite nothing, I do want something

AKMED

What?

DAVE

Your soul!

SHAMIA

My soul! That belongs to Allah.

DAVE

And what is he going to give you for it?

AKMED

Dozens of vestal virgins to start with.

DAVE

And is that guaranteed?

AKMED

Cautiously and with some apparent reservation.

Yes.

DAVE

What I am offering you can have now, and you don't have to die to get it!

SHAMIA
So, what exactly is my soul?

DAVE
It's what you are right now, today, at this very moment. If you died right now, what is left is the bit that I take, the bit you won't need anymore.

SHAMIA
If I was dead, I wouldn't know.

DAVE
Precisely, but with my offer, you wouldn't have to die right now. We could agree on mutually agreeable terms for your departure sometime in the future.

SHAMIA
Sounds like an offer where everyone wins.

DAVE
In a manner of speaking, it is.

AKMED
And what do we actually get?

DAVE

As I said, it's negotiable, but you could have fame, money, or both, even your vestal virgins and time, lots of extra time. We would just have to come to an arrangement on the completion period for the contract.

AKMED

So, I could be world-famous and wealthy.

DAVE

Yes, or you could continue to be a freedom fighter

WALTER

Terrorist

Akmed throws Walter a withering scowl.

DAVE

And spend the extra time killing whoever you like with total invincibility, and you could blow yourselves up as many times as you like if you wanted to.

SHAMIA

So, we could become the greatest freedom fighters of all time?

DAVE

Absolutely, and not die, and the added bonus is you will stay the same age forever, more or less. You would never grow old, and you have the virgins now. They are becoming increasingly rare these days.

AKMED

And I get to keep my good looks despite exploding occasionally

DAVE

Absolutely.

AKMED

And what sort of completion period are we talking about?

DAVE

Forty years, what about that?

AKMED

That's not long.

DAVE

It's better than your current life expectancy, which according to my information, is three months if you're lucky, but you do get to keep your soul and a tenuous promise of some treats in the afterlife.

Akmed throws Dave an inquisitorial expression.

SHAMIA

I would only be sixty-seven.

DAVE

That's higher than the average for the really famous and wealthy. Only a few scrape by with anything much longer, and they are mainly the do-gooders and coffin dodgers…

You know Jesus, Mohammed, Mother Teresa, Cliff Richards. We occasionally make an exception for them. But in the main, it's your Presley, Hendrix, Holly, Lennon, Monroe, Morrison, Mercury types.

AKMED

How come you don't need our souls straight away.

DAVE

I'm not a desperate man. I have a few in stock at the moment.

SHAMIA

In stock, what, you have like a warehouse full of unused souls?

DAVE

Not quite a warehouse as such, more of a 'stock in transit situation,' with a specific delivery date if you see what I mean. But yes, I do have a few in reserve for emergencies.

SHAMIA

Emergencies? What, you mean if you feel a bit peckish, you get one out of the freezer and bang it into the microwave for dinner.

DAVE

I don't eat them, for God's sake, I'm not a cannibal. I'm a vegan, actually. I just need them to rejuvenate my soul, which becomes a bit depleted over time with all the good work I have to do. If I didn't have a soul, I would die, which would be a catastrophe for me and the world. Peace and harmony would break out everywhere. Everyone would be happy and smiling and content. It would be absolutely dreadful; just the thought of it makes me want to throw up.

MORGIANA

Abruptly

Some might say that wouldn't be such a bad thing.

Shamia and Akmed turn to Morgiana, who has been intently listening to their conversation. She has realised who Dave is.

DAVE

Turns to Morgiana

I'm not the worst thing in the world. There are some people out there a lot nastier than me.

Dave gestures to the noise outside.

That's not my bag. It's all a bit indiscriminate for my liking; it has that unsavoury whiff of servile Presbyterianism about it…

Everybody looks at Dave; they appear confused.

Doing evil things for the better good. That's not for me. It sounds a little underhand and hypocritical to me.

MORGIANA

Some people might argue that.

DAVE

Only religious zealots, the real evil in the world, comes from within.

He turns back at Akmed and Shamia

So, what do you think about my offer?

SHAMIA

You said we could have anything?

DAVE

That's right

SHAMIA

Absolutely anything?

DAVE

Anything at all, but you can't cancel the contract after we've struck a deal.

SHAMIA

Money?

DAVE

Yes, I told you that.

MORGIANA

Fame?

Dave turns to look at Morgiana.

DAVE

I didn't think you were interested.

MORGIANA

Why not?

DAVE

Because women nearly always turn me down in the end, they become all virtuous and holier than thou, so I don't bother asking.

MORGIANA

I wonder why that is?

She says this sarcastically.

DAVE

Who knows?

AKMED

What about power? Will I get that?

DAVE

That's a tricky one. Everybody wants power, but if I give it to everybody equally, that dissipates its value.
There is a natural declension in the worth of a shared intangible. I can provide a little power here and there, but nothing absolute that would be like giving up my throne….

Dave smiles

MORGIANA

Would I find a decent husband?

DAVE

Now you are having a laugh. I can give you access to any man, but you must play it out as best you see fit. I'm not a miracle worker.

SHAMIA

Do we get a contract?

DAVE

If you insist... but no lawyers to check it over. I haven't got that sort of time to waste.

SHAMIA

So, what do we do now?

DAVE

You don't have to do anything, not until tomorrow, that's when I need a decision, but it must be both of you. I can't take one brother without the other, don't like to break up siblings. It sends out bad vibes, and my legal department is strangely averse to negative Karma. Oh, and Morgiana…

MORGIANA

Yes?

DAVE

You can come along for the ride if you want.

MORGIANA

You're all heart.

Dave smiles

AKMED

What if we have more questions?

DAVE

I'll answer them tomorrow.

SHAMIA

Right. So, we'll see you tomorrow at…?

DAVE

Six. I will be back at six o'clock, and now I will bid you good night.

SHAMIA

One more question.

DAVE

Yes

SHAMIA

What about them?

He points at Dizzie, JJ, Walter and Ali

Why don't you want theirs?

DAVE

It's a good question, but they aren't on my shortlist of current potentials, and I don't like bad press.

He laughs at the irony.

SHAMIA

On your list? You have a list?

DAVE

Of course, and I have a filing system - just in case anybody declines, a lot do rather oddly. Oh, and I already have Ali's soul, had it for ages…

He waves at Dave, and Dave waves back in acknowledgement.

That's why your gun didn't work in here. He's protected. He has one of the earlier contracts. They were very generous back then.

He points up at the sign stating when the business was established. Everybody looks at the sign, and a sudden realisation overtakes them.

SHAMIA

Oh.

Dave leaves through the exit door, and the room goes quiet.

SHAMIA

Okay, so what about the space travelling loony?

AKMED

I don't think he's a loony, but we will soon know if he doesn't come back tomorrow.

They both turn and look at Ali as if to ask his opinion.

ALI

He is a redemptor, I can vouch for that much, and the deal is working okay for me… so far.

AKMED

So, let's just assume he's hasn't fried his brain in the sun?

SHAMIA

I'm going for a piss.

AKMED

Amazing. We reach a pivotal point in our very existence, one that could change our lives forever, and all you want to do is go for a piss instead of discussing the possibility of immortality.

SHAMIA

I could stand here and chat if you like, but I would have to piss on the floor.

Shamia wanders out through one of the exit doors

AKMED

We could all piss on the floor, I suppose. It may not make a lot of difference after tomorrow.

ALI

I'd rather you didn't. I'll still have to clean it up after you've gone.

AKMED

So, Ali, how long did you get?

DAVE

Reluctantly

It was early days back then. There weren't too many takers, so I managed to get two thousand years, but no fame or fortune, just time.

WALTER

Wow, some deal.

ALI

It was then, but that was 17AD

AKMED

So, that means your time is nearly up…

ALI

Next year, that's right.

WALTER

Not so good then.

Ali holds his hands out, palm upwards as if to say, "That's life."

Shakira enters through the centre door. Everybody watches her as she takes a seat at the bar.

ALI

Hi Shakira, how are you doing?

SHAKIRA

So, so, I looking for Shamia, have you seen him recently?

Ali looks around at the other customers

ALI

Has anybody seen Shamia?

CAST

General mutterings of "No."

AKMED

Smirking

He did say something about popping out to see some celestial virgins, I think…

SHAKIRA

Sharply

If he thinks he blows him fuck self-up and bugger off to screw hordes of bloody virgins, he's got another think coming. It's my pottery class tonight, and he's looking after Abdulla.

AKMED

Only joking Shakira, he's in the bog having a piss.

SHAKIRA

He better be fucking pissing, or I blow his fucking dick off. One day, Akmed, I'll cut your tiny dick off if I can find it.

She smiles, Akmed looks concerned.
Everybody else laughs and make little penis gestures.

SHAMIA

Shamia reappears through the main door

Mashallah!

Shamia exclaims, throwing his arms up

It's a vision from heaven, hello my dearest beloved.

SHAKIRA

Don't you dearest beloved me, dickhead. They tell me you popping off and fucking celestial tarts.

SHAMIA

Not me dear, that's all religious dogma and propaganda… alchemy of the Gods, they're just having a laugh, you are buggers you lot.

Shamia castigates the others by half-heartedly waving a finger at them and flashing an angry expression.

AKMED

Sorry bro' sorry Shakira, I was only joking. You know you are my favourite little sister-in-law. I wouldn't upset you for the world.

Shakira flashes a searing expression at Akmed. Akmed flinches back a few inches.

SHAKIRA

Don't think you can get around me that easily. You are arsehole Akmed. I hope a sniper shoot your balls off.

AKMED

Ooooh, charming.

He clenches his crotch

Shamia and Shakira make to leave the bar.

SHAMIA

We're off then, see you lot around five tomorrow.

ALI

See you tomorrow Shaky.

Everybody else waves and bids farewell.

WALTER

God willing

SHAMIA

Allah willing

Walter smiles.
Shamia and Shakira leave.

MORGIANA

To Ali

So, you've already done a deal with him?

ALI

With the Redemptor, yes.

He continues polishing glasses.

MORGIANA

So, was it worth it?

ALI

Yes, I think so, but I don't know how it ends yet. That will be the surprise.

AKMED

Emm.

WALTER

I'm going back to the base, are you coming?

DIZZIE

Well no.

WALTER

No?

DIZZIE

No, not just yet.

WALTER

But we always go back to base together.

DIZZIE

Only because you don't drive.

WALTER

But you always drive.

DIZZIE

Exactly, I do everything. It's always the same.
Can you check the E.N.G. Diz?
Can you check the transmission connection rate Diz?
Can you check the satellite link, Diz?
Can you drive me home, Diz?
Can you make sure my nose doesn't look too big on screen?
Can you wipe my arse Diz?
Well, I have had it up to here! You check the bloody equipment, and you drive back. I've got something more important to think about, and I'm staying here for a while, and what's more, when that looney tune turns up tomorrow, I'm might just ask him if I can have one of these deals.

WALTER

You've never mentioned this before. I didn't know you felt like this.

DIZZIE

You've never asked, you've never been remotely interested in me or how I feel, you…

WALTER

Hey, Walter, look, I'm sorry, I didn't realise.

DIZZIE

I listened to what Dave said, and do you know what, there must be a better life than this. I have been with you for three bloody years. By your side through thick and thin, night and day never argued with you once, always made sure you don't go out dressed like a prat, always made sure you've got clean pants on.

You get the right food for your nut allergy, and you take your heart pills every night, even when you're pissed. I clean up the puke when you throw up all over the room.

CONT

DIZZIE CONT...

I do your washing, drying, I iron your shirts, trousers and even your bloody skiddies, and I never, never say anything about you having the biggest conk I've ever seen.

And what thanks do I get? Nothing, not a sausage, not diddley squat. And when this Dave dude comes along and says he can change the world... my world, do you even bother to ask my opinion? No! No need to because you've already sold your fucking soul to CNN, so you're laughing, and I've been left behind yet again. Well, not this time.

This time, I am going to bugger off and get pissed and give some serious consideration about having a chat with Dave when he comes back tomorrow about getting a contract, so you can walk home and lump it.

WALTER

Now steady on Diz, it is a good job, and you do get paid well for it.

DIZZIE

They don't pay me enough to get shot at every day.

WALTER

But it's what we do.

DIZZIE

Oh, it's we now. Why is it that every time we go on air, all the world ever sees is you? You've been here, you've seen this, you've done that.
Nobody ever wonders about who is actually holding the camera and controlling the sound, getting everything just right so you look just so. While you're looking around and describing the incoming missiles that are whistling over your head, my only concern is that while my head is bent over looking through a lens making sure you look good, at any moment, a rocket may just disappear up my arse. But do I complain? No. I just get on and do it, but I've had enough.

WALTER

Diz, I'm sorry, I never thought that…

DIZZIE

That's the trouble you never think; you just react. My problem is I think too much and worry too much. I'm just not instinctive like you.

WALTER

I can empathise with you on that, especially if you spend half your day expecting a large delivery through the back door.

Walter sniggers.
Dizzie is not impressed.

DIZZIE

I'm concerned about you as well as me.

WALTER

Walter leans over and kisses Dizzie on the head

I can see that. I never knew you cared. Come on, I'll drive you home.

DIZZIE

But you can't drive.

He looks surprised.

WALTER

Can't drive, who told you that? I just never bothered to mention it before, but as you've asked.

They gather up their equipment and begin to leave.

DIZZIE

It's all right. I'll drive. I am the driver.

WALTER

Whatever you want, Diz, you're in charge.

DIZZIE

Am I?

WALTER

Is my nose really that big?

DIZZIE

No, not really; I'm sorry about that; I was just a little bit peeved.

WALTER

Peeved?

DIZZIE

Deep down, I am a passionate person, you know

WALTER

Oh, I can see that.

Walter and Dizzie leave with all their equipment. Walking out through the exit doors holding hands.

AKMED

And they call us camel shaggers. At least we don't fuck our friends.

ALI

We all fuck our friends, one way or another, in the end.

AKMED

Well, I think Walters been a bit of a shit,

ALI

Akmed, mate, you just haven't seen enough of the world yet. Take my word, it's a lot worse than you think.

AKMED

So, what are you going to do?

ALI

Me, nothing. I don't have to do anything.

AKMED

So, you really have sold your soul to Dave?

ALI

Yes, well, not Dave, exactly, but one of his associates… they have a sort of job-sharing arrangement, hot desking for Soul Traders Incorporated if you like.

Ali smiles and continues polishing a glass.

JJ

That's why he turned up here because he knows you?

ALI

He must know I have a contract.

MORGIANA

So why aren't you living the high life, more to the point, why are you living in a shithouse like this.

She throws her arms and flashes an expression indicating the bar is a dump

ALI

That's a bit harsh.

Ali takes benign offence at Morgiana's remark

It is steady work, and it is my bar and home, and anyway, I'm here because I like it, and it keeps me entertained. But a couple of thousand years is a long time to be on your own in the same place, so I like to move around a bit, meet new people. Anyway, worldwide fame didn't exist back then, they didn't have a Big Jerusalem Bake-off or Jordan's Got Talent, so the extra years seemed a good idea.

JJ

But you're not on your own; you have us.

ALI

Yes, but even you will all grow old and die,

CONT

ALI CONT…

or have families and drift away… or get blown up for a good cause…
but I will still be here, the same age as I always was, making new friends; I didn't think about that in the beginning. So now I have to make the best fist of it I can.

He continues polishing his beer glasses.

AKMED

How old are you?

ALI

Let me think… I must be about a couple of thousand years old now, would you believe.

AKMED

Wow… you look good.

Morgiana and JJ look at Akmed with stunned amazement.

MORGIANA

He's older than he looks, Akmed.

AKMED

I know that!

Akmed responds abruptly with a hint of indignation

MORGIANA

I bet you've seen a lot of changes.

ALI

A few.

MORGIANA

So, was it all worth it?

ALI

Worth what?

MORGIANA

Doing the deal, taking the package…?

ALI

I really don't know to be honest. I only have a few years to go before my contract is up; maybe I'll know by then, but it has been interesting. One thing I can tell you, and that is nothing much changes in the way people kill each other. It is more inventive now but just as destructive as it's always been. Why do you ask?

MORGIANA

I was wondering whether it was worth asking for myself, so I need to know if it's a good deal before I…

ALI

I think he offers a lot more these days. All I got was this bar, a couple of thousand years and a dog.

MORGIANA

Where's the dog

ALI

It died of old age, quite a few times. The Redemptor forgot to mention that bit.

JJ

What about getting married and having children?

ALI

I have been happily married about thirty times; each wife lasted for around forty years. They have all gone. All the children have grown up, grown old and died. I didn't have any children last time; I was beginning to get a bit depressed at losing everybody and moving on alone. It's all a bit sad, really.

MORGIANA

I'm sorry.

ALI

Nothing to be sorry for. They all had a good run. It was me that carried on while they just quietly faded away. Back to being on my own, I prefer it that way now.

MORGIANA

So, immortality's not all it's cracked up to be?

ALI

That all depends on you and what you want.

MORGIANA

Emm.

JJ

I'm going home, do you want me to walk with you, Max?

MORGIANA

That would be nice, JJ.

JJ

What about you Akmed?

AKMED

I'm going the other way. I got a few surprises for you tonight.

JJ

Thanks for the warning.

AKMED

I'll see you all tomorrow

JJ

Hope so.

They all leave, and Ali is left clearing up the glasses and tidying up the bar.

SECOND HALF

THE FOLLOWING DAY AROUND 4.00 PM.

Walter, Dizzie and JJ enter wearing bandages over minor wounds. JJ, looking very distressed, is limping on a crutch with his umbrella tied to it. They all sit down at a table.
Akmed is sitting at the bar near the exit door quietly drinking a coke.
Ali is standing at the bar polishing a glass and smoking a cigar. He spits in the spittoon.
Morgiana is sitting at the other end of the bar drinking a cocktail.
Shamia enters, brandishing his AK47 above his head. He bumps his gun into the door frame over his head, mutters Fuck!

SHAMIA

As salamu ‘alaykum wa rahmatullaahi
we barakato.
Death to all infidels and non-believers!

Nobody takes any notice except Ali. He drops the cloth, looks directly at Shamia and promptly raises his open hand again as if reprimanding him.

ALI

Christ Shaky, I told you yesterday not so much noise; Everybody is trying to have a quiet drink after all that noise last night.

SHAMIA

Sorry, Ali, a force of habit… we had a good night, so I feel like celebrating.

WALTER

Well, we don't. You hit the communication hut. I was just having a cup of hot chocolate and bosh, suddenly the hut was gone.

JJ

And the sky… the sky was gone.

He speaks slowly and appears grief-stricken as he speaks. He holds his hands up to the heavens.

The cast, mystified by JJ's emotive muttering, look at Walter for some explanation.

WALTER

Sky TV… he's passionate about baseball.

The cast now understands and commiserate.

SHAMIA

Look, I'm sorry about that, it's nothing personal.

Shamia appears oddly apologetic.

WALTER

So, you should be. Creeping up in the dark, throwing rockets at us from all directions.

SHAMIA

We have to do it in the dark so that we can surprise your lot. They shoot back in the daytime if they see us.

DIZZIE

It's not cricket, and I don't like surprises. Just look at poor JJ. He is mortified.

WALTER

I don't like surprises either. I was just nodding off when the first rocket landed.

SHAMIA

I am sorry, I'll send a text next time, give you a bit of warning…

Everybody looks at Shamia

Well, maybe not a text, only trying to be helpful.

JJ, Walter and Dizzie glare at Shamia. JJ waves his crutch

MORGIANA

So, have you two decided?

There is some general muttering between Akmed and Shamia –

SHAMIA

Well, Akmed and I have discussed this matter long and hard last night and/

WALTER

Interrupts

/In between launching rockets at us.

SHAMIA

I have apologised.

WALTER

Mutters something incomprehensible

SHAMIA

…and after much consideration, we have decided… yes. We are going to take the deal, subject to a few conditions. On balance, we think it would be a good decision. It means we will become wealthy and famous, and we can carry on fighting the infidels for at least another forty years, so it's a win-win for us.

MORGIANA

Morgiana looks surprised

So, you are selling your souls to the Redemptor just so you can carry on killing people with impunity and become rich and famous at the same time. That sounds like an incredibly moronic decision without the tiniest shred of integrity. I really don't think you've thought it through at all.

SHAMIA

Well, you would think that, wouldn't you…? You're a woman, so you couldn't possibly understand how a man's mind works.

MORGIANA

You've got me there.

pause

So, what does Shakira think about this plan?

SHAMIA

Well, I haven't actually mentioned it to Shakira yet, but I'm sure the money will bring her around to my way of thinking.

MORGIANA

That's what you think, is it?

SHAMIA

Yes.

MORGIANA

Aren't you happy with the life you have right now, with Shakira and baby Abdulla?

SHAMIA

Yes. Of course, I am, but I need to develop my career and move forward with my progressive business plan's long-term strategy, which this move will do very quickly.

MORGIANA

Being a terrorist is hardly a long-term proposal, and it's definitely not a good career move.

AKMED

We are freedom fighters, not terrorists, and freedom fighters eventually become politicians.

MORGIANA

Fuck me, they are more corrupt than terrorists.

AKMED

I will be an honest politician.

WALTER

Laughs

No such animal.

AKMED

Directed at Morgiana

I will be good politician.

MORGIANA

Whatever.

Morgiana pauses for a moment

Let me tell you a little story Akmed - before you finally make the decision.

SHAMIA

Please do, but I don't think it will change our minds.

The lights dim, and there is just a spotlight on Morgiana.

MORGIANA

This is a story which you will probably all know some, but not all. It's about Ali Baba and his elder brother Cassim, the two sons of a merchant in Persia and the forty thieves.

After their father's death, Cassim marries a wealthy woman and becomes even richer building up his father's business, but he never has quite enough money and is always looking for more.

CONT...

MORGIANA CONT…

Ali Baba, however, never marries and settles into the trade of a humble woodcutter, and he is happy.
One day, Ali Baba is out collecting firewood in the forest when he stumbles on a group of forty thieves visiting their secret treasure store. The treasure is in a cave, the mouth of which opens and closes with two magic words.

After the thieves have gone, Ali Baba uses the magic words and enters the cave. He takes a single bag of gold coins' home, enough for all his needs for many years. But his brother, Cassim, finds out about the gold and under pressure from his brother, Ali Baba is forced to reveal the secret of the cave.

Although already very rich, Cassim goes to the cave, taking a donkey with him to steal as much treasure as he can carry. He enters the cave with the magic words, but in his greed and excitement, he forgets the words to let him out and finds himself trapped. Later that night, the thieves return, see him there and kill him.

CONT…

MORGIANA CONT…

When his brother does not come back, Ali Baba goes to the cave to look for him and finds his body quartered with each piece displayed just inside the cave's entrance to warn anyone else who might try to enter.

The whole cast is now engrossed in Morgiana's retelling of the story.

Ali Baba brings the body home, where he entrusts Morgiana, a clever slave-girl from Cassim's household,

Morgiana smiles at everybody and points two fingers at herself.

with the task of making Cassim look as though he died a natural death. Morgiana finds an old tailor whom she pays, blindfolds, and leads to Cassim's house.

There, overnight, the tailor stitches the pieces of Cassim's body back together so that no one will be suspicious, and Ali Baba and his family can give Cassim a proper burial without anyone asking awkward questions.

CONT…

MORGIANA

Now the thieves, finding the body gone, realize that yet another person must know their secret, and they set out to track him down. They eventually find out that Ali Baba knows the cave's secret, and they plan to kill him.

The leader of the thieves pretends to be an oil merchant in need of Ali Baba's hospitality, bringing with him mules loaded with 40 oil jars, one filled with oil, the other 39 hiding the other remaining thieves.

Once Ali Baba is asleep, the thieves plan to kill him. Once again, Morgiana discovers and foils the plan, killing the 39 thieves in their oil jars by pouring boiling oil on them. When their leader comes to rouse his men, he discovers they are all dead and he escapes.

The following day, Morgiana tells Ali Baba about the thieves in the jars. They bury them, and Ali Baba shows his gratitude by giving Morgiana her freedom.

CONT…

MORGIANA
To exact revenge, the leader of the thieves establishes himself as a merchant and befriends Ali Baba's son (who is now in charge of the late Cassim's business), and is invited to dinner at Ali Baba's house.

However, the thief is recognized by Morgiana, who performs a sword dance with a dagger for the diners and then suddenly plunges it into the thief's heart when he is off his guard. Ali Baba is angry at first with Morgiana, but when he finds out the thief wanted to kill him, he is very grateful. Then he realizes he is in love with Morgiana, and he asks her to marry him.

Ali Baba is then left as the only one knowing the secret of the treasure in the cave and how to access it. But he never bothers going back because the treasure has brought so much sadness to his family. So, he just lives his life quietly with Morgiana and their children, but he always remembers what happened to his brother Cassim who wanted too much and lost everything.

The cast gently applauds

SHAMIA

And your point is?

MORGIANA

Well, I like to think of you as Ali Baba having a good life with Shakira and baby Abdulla. However, if you take this deal, you may become a greedy Cassim, or worse still, the leader of the forty thieves or freedom fighters in your case/

WALTER

Terrorists!

Shamia grudgingly acknowledges Walter

MORGIANA

/And they all die in the end.

Everybody nods

I suppose what I am trying to say is you may be about to receive the key to a cave full of gold, and you may live forever, but at what cost?

SHAMIA

As I said, it was a nice story, but you haven't convinced me to change my mind. And we do get immortality thrown in, so we can't die.

He looks at Akmed, who shakes his head in agreement.

MORGIANA

All right then, try this one. Have you heard the theory about the monkeys, typewriters, Shakespeare, and time?

SHAMIA

I've heard it.

MORGIANA

So, holding that thought, let me put this to you. Suppose life has a master plan, a plan that dictates everything that happens, every moment of the day for everyone then surely there is no question; There must be a god, the person who designed the plan and controls everything that happens in it and therefore it is preordained. In that case, it could be Allah or a Christian god whoever. Do you agree?

SHAMIA

reluctantly

Yes… I suppose so.

MORGIANA

Good. Now consider this. What if there was no plan and life was just an incalculable number of random actions that happen every second to everybody like an enormous lottery that we all subscribe to every second of every day, and everything that happens to us is simply the outcome of luck, destiny, happenchance, or serendipity and whether you even take another breath is governed by this lottery of life, then surely that would prove there was no god?

SHAMIA

I'm not sure about that one. Allah is God.

MORGIANA

Fair enough, so let me elaborate just a little further and ask you these questions; who organised this lottery? Who runs this lottery every second, every day; it's a giant lottery, so it would take a gigantic computer or something even more significant than that; maybe a god could run this lottery of life, but if there is no god, who is running it? How does everything that happens happen?

SHAMIA

I don't know.

MORGIANA

That's my point. We don't know. It's all taken on trust without any evidence.
So, if you are prepared to take that chance and believe wholeheartedly, as you do, in Allah or whoever is up there when there is no supportive evidence of his existence, then why jeopardise everything for a deal with the Anti-Allah, because that's who Dave is. All he is offering for your soul is just a little bit of immortality.
But what do you really get? Look at our landlord, Ali, he didn't really get extra time - he got an incredibly long life sentence and for what?
So, the question is, are you an Ali Baba or a Cassim?

Shamia looks at Akmed, and they acknowledge that what Morgiana is saying makes sense. They both look over at Ali, who is polishing a tumbler, and he flashes them an expression as if to say, "she could be right" they then glance at Dizzie, Walter and JJ, who do much the same. Then they look back at Morgiana.

SHAMIA

So, who are you… really? The person with all the wise words.

MORGIANA

Ah, now that would be telling, but what I can tell you is I am nobody special... my husband is a carpet seller, and he's a bit of a bastard, and he will shag anything on legs but, let me tell you this……

Morgiana puts her arms out to embrace Akmed and Shamia.

The three wander out through the main central doors, and Morgiana whispers something to Shamia and Akmed. They laugh out aloud. Dizzie, JJ and Walter raise their glasses to make a toast, and Ali continues polishing a glass as the lights fade away.
George Michael song "They Won't Go When I Go" begins to play on the jukebox.

THE END

I know this is not perfect by any means, but I am working on it every day, so it will get better.

Printed in Great Britain
by Amazon

82866421R00098